Something To Crow About

Written By **Richard A. Klein**

Illustrated By **Ariel M. Coburn**

ARPress
45 Dan Road Suite 5
Canton MA 02021

Hotline: 1(888) 821-0229
Fax: 1(508) 545-7580

Ordering Information:

Quantity sales. Special discounts are available on quantity purchases by corporations, associations, and others. For details, contact the publisher at the address above.

Printed in the United States of America.

ISBN-13:   Softcover   979-8-89389-849-1
             eBook   979-8-89389-850-7
Library of Congress Control Number: 2024923725

SOMETHING TO CROW ABOUT

RICHARD A. KLEIN

Moe The Crow was black from head to toe.
He was young and curious—and sometimes even furious

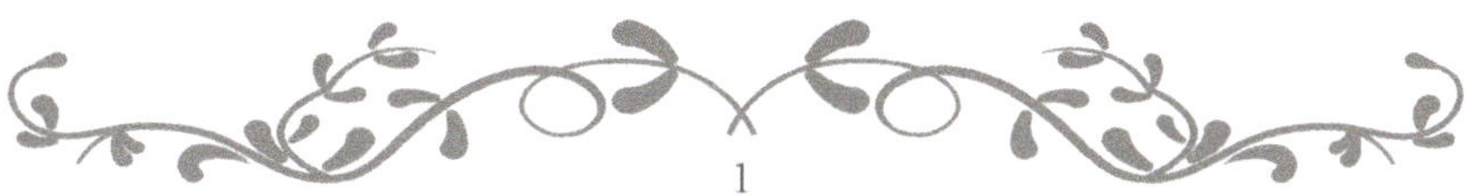

He was small, not tall, really at all,
And stuck in a tree as high as could be.

**From his tree, a birch, he would gaze from his perch
Looking below at the constant flow of those not crow:**

Girls with curls, boys with toys—all seemed to enjoy Having a ball, growing up tall, as large as a wall.

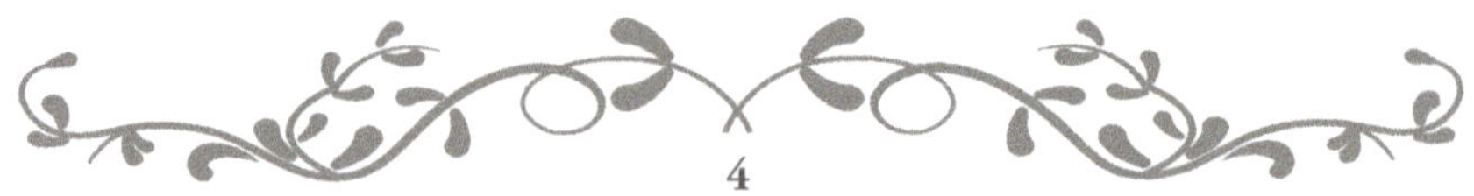

What about me—stuck in a tree—such a little peewee?
I hate to be whiny, but I'm so puny and tiny.

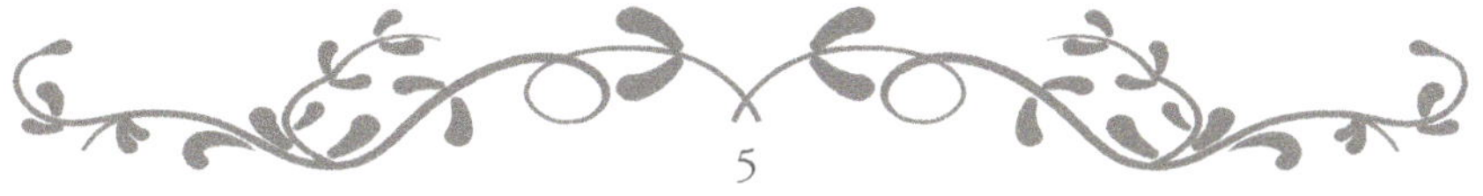

I'm just a little bird, as everyone has heard;
The future doesn't look good ahead if I stay like this, he said.

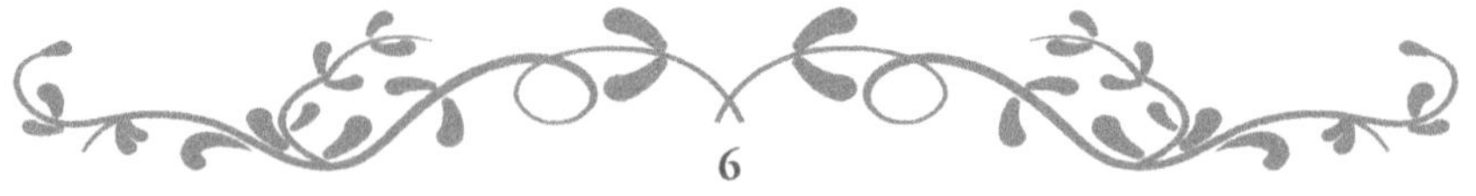

At least he was a bird who would soon fly through the sky.
He was bigger than the bee flying with glee close to the tree.

**I wish I had been born big instead of as little as a twig.
Was my family always so small and never really tall?**

Mama bird heard all this and gave young Moe a kiss.
You are beautiful and black and you should now think back

**To a time long ago when we were not always a crow:
Some of us were tall as trees, like a very different species.**

**It was back many a year that we did first appear,
And everyone would fear what all could loudly hear:**

The sound and roar of the mighty dinosaur
Shaking the earth's floor—he was the beast of lore.

He was as tall as a tree, as big as could be.
None could match his girth anywhere on earth.

Dinosaurs were tough as granite and ran the entire planet.
They had teeth and a tail, and they were as large as a whale.

Our family factor says our origin was a microraptor.
Fine feathers we all sported, or so it was reported.

Millions of years we have been alive and full of drive,
Evolving from microraptor to a whole new word: the bird.

We started out in late Jurassic to become a classic of what we are today: a crow in every way.

Although we had no choice, we kept a loud voice;
No longer a roar, but something more raw: our familiar crow caw.

**Our great size did not last, but always remember your past
When your ancestors did roam, and the earth was their home.**

We never did lack glorious feathers on our back
Which we gladly display while flying far away.

Moe the crow was black from head to toe.
And now full of pride of the feathers on his hide.

Always mischievous and curious, he grew more serious About life gone by and his future in the sky.

His eyes were blue: a juvenile hue.
Moe would frown when they turned dark brown.

At life's every turn, he would be quick to learn
How to follow the rules, including making bird tools.

Moe the Crow would continue to grow from head to toe; Making the most of his days in so many new ways.

**The proudest bird in the tree as everyone can clearly see;
It is now said: surely life's best is what lies ahead.**

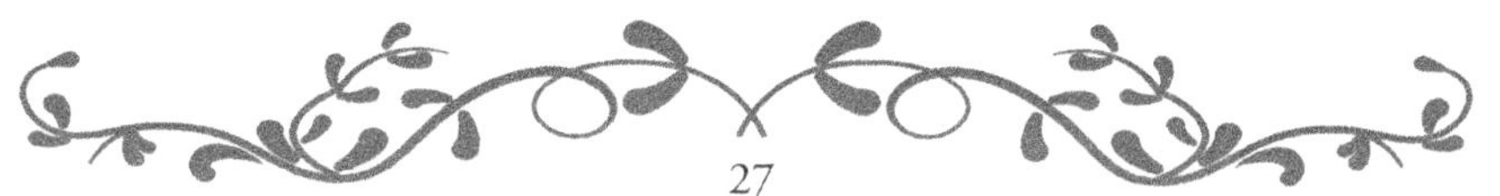